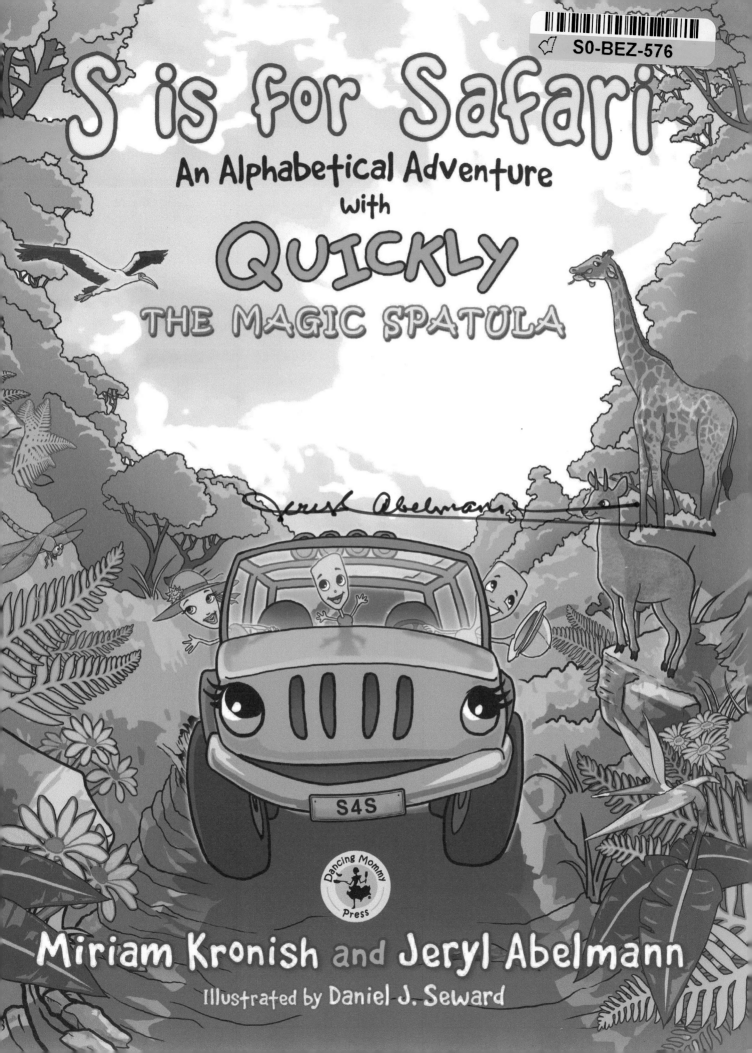

S is for Safari

An Alphabetical Adventure
with
QUICKLY
THE MAGIC SPATULA

S4S

Miriam Kronish and Jeryl Abelmann
Illustrated by Daniel J. Seward

S is for Safari

An Alphabetical Adventure with Quickly the Magic Spatula

For information or to order additional copies please contact:

Dancing Mommy Press
P.O. Box 321
Pebble Beach, CA 93953
www.DancingMommyPress.com

Designed and Illustrated by Daniel J. Seward.
The Pannekoek recipe by Jackie Pelletier reprinted with kind permission.

Visit us on the web:
www.QuicklyTheMagicSpatula.com
www.SisForSafari.com

Names: Kronish, Miriam, author. | Abelmann, Jeryl, author. | Seward, Daniel J., illustrator.
Title: S is for safari : an alphabetical adventure with Quickly the Magic Spatula / Miriam Kronish and Jeryl Abelmann ; illustrated by Daniel J. Seward.
Description: First edition. | Pebble Beach, CA : Dancing Mommy Press, [2016] | Statement of responsibility from cover. | Audience: Ages 4-8. |
Summary: Quickly the Magic Spatula goes on an alphabetical safari to South Africa.--Publisher.
Identifiers: SBN: 978-0-9971084-6-0 (pbk.) | 978-0-9971084-7-7 (hardcover) | 978-0-9971084-8-4 | (ebook) | LCCN: 2016936341
Subjects: LCSH: Alphabet books. | Animals--South Africa--Juvenile literature. | Safaris--South Africa--Juvenile fiction. | Kitchen utensils--Juvenile fiction.
| Adventure and adventurers--Juvenile fiction. | CYAC: Alphabet books. | Animals--South Africa. | Safaris--South Africa--Fiction. | Kitchen utensils--Fiction.
| Adventure and adventurers--Fiction. | Voyages and travels--Fiction. | LCGFT: Alphabet rhymes. |
BISAC: JUVENILE FICTION / Action & Adventure / General.
Classification: LCC: PZ7.K92285 S14 2016 | DDC: E--dc23

Printed in the USA
2 4 6 8 9 7 5 3 1
First edition

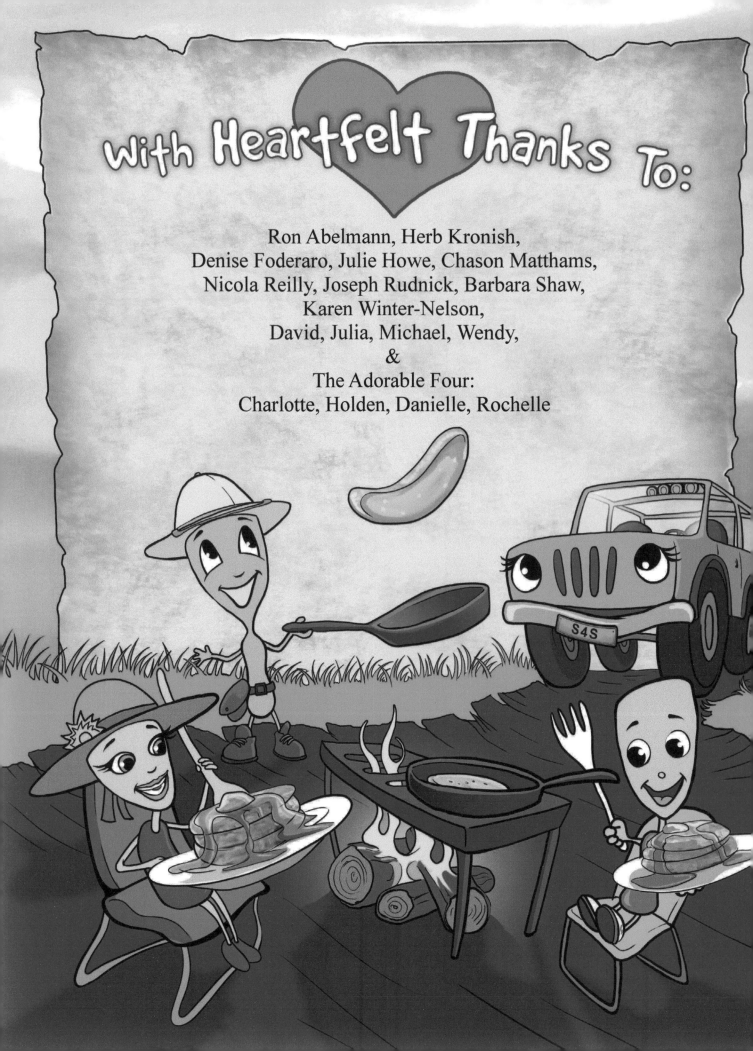

With Heartfelt Thanks To:

Ron Abelmann, Herb Kronish,
Denise Foderaro, Julie Howe, Chason Matthams,
Nicola Reilly, Joseph Rudnick, Barbara Shaw,
Karen Winter-Nelson,
David, Julia, Michael, Wendy,
&
The Adorable Four:
Charlotte, Holden, Danielle, Rochelle

Hello!
I'm Quickly, the Magic Spatula,
And I'm thrilled to say,
We're going on safari with our friends today.

PanDora and I met Ponnie last year.
Ponnie lives in South Africa
And invited us here.
We're visiting the animals and learning their names.
We're seeing the country and playing some games.
So let's find an animal that starts with **A**
Just turn the page and we're on our way!

South Africa's national animal starts with
It's an antelope and
We shout, "Hooray!"
In the antelope family
There are many different kinds.
This one's called a springbok.
It runs fast and then unwinds.

B stands for buffalo, one of the Big Five.

If you look at its back, you'll find a tiny bird.

No, it's not absurd to find a bird on the buffalo's back.

The oxpecker is its name.

What a wonderful word!

And the Cape buffalo loves to be part of a herd.

We're on to the next letter and it's a
We're looking at a cheetah, covered with spots,
Lots and lots of darkish dots.

The cheetah is the fastest cat.
No other animal can run like that.

4

Dragonfly begins with D
It's the next thing that we see.
A dragonfly sparkles with colors that delight —
Orange, green, and violet catch the light.

Here comes another of the Big Five.
It's an elephant with its very long trunk,
And enormous ears to brush bugs away
And keep it cool on a long, hot day.

What a thrilling sight —
To view this animal both day and night.
It's plain to see the letter E

F fills our sights with a flock of flamingos.
Their tongues are long and sticky —
No, that's not icky!
Sticky tongues catch insects for these birds.
They also eat water plants
And even ants.

The giraffe is next on our safari —

A very tall

It loves to feed on the leaves of the acacia tree.
We watch it walk so gracefully.

As we stand on the bank of a river,
The hippopotamus comes into view.

H stands for hippo —
Hippos love to play in the water.
Don't you think they oughtta?

brings us to the impala,
We watch it bound,
Deftly darting all around,
And it hardly makes a sound.

J

Jackals start with a J
How they love to run and play,
And go on sleeping through the day.
In the darkness of the night,
That is when they come in sight.

The next animal we see is the tiny klipspringer.

What a humdinger!

Klipspringers love to climb on rocks and up hills.

Their daring feats, their daily drills

Afford us thrills,

And give us our letter 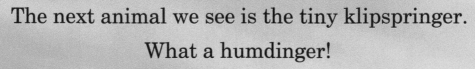 K today.

L includes the lion and the leopard —
Two more of the Big Five.
Lions love to nap in their lairs.
Leopards lie in wait in trees,
Listening to the whispering breeze.
The leopard's spots, the lion's mane,
Our quest to see them will never wane.

Monkeys are so much fun to watch
As they go about their day,
Frolicking and climbing as they may,
Among the flowers
By the hours.
Monkeys begin with M

Good for them!

Nagapies have great big eyes.
They sleep by day and come out at night.
Their nickname is bushbaby.
You'll realize why
When you hear their cry.
N is for the name nagapie.

Oh my!
We spy an **O**strich running in the wild.
This gigantic bird lays the largest eggs
And has the longest legs.
In a race, its feathers will leave you in the dust —
Trust my word!

P is for penguins, so nattily dressed.

They parade, they promenade,

They pose so prettily.

The picture-perfect pair — so there!

We now come to the letter Q
What are we to do?
"Ah, I know, says PanDora with a smile,
There are even Q's on your shoes!
The Q will stand for **you** —

QUICKLY!"

We are now at the letter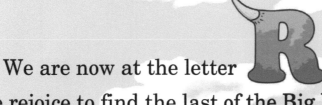
And we rejoice to find the last of the Big Five —
The rhinoceros!
We see this huge animal on the road,
So much huger than a toad.

Let's review the really Big Five:
Buffalo, elephant, lion, leopard, and lastly,
The rhinoceros.
One, two, three, four, five —
We found our game
And know their names!

S is for Safari —

And now you know what a safari is:

A trip to discover the flora and fauna,

The plants and animals,

The sights and sounds

That abound all around us.

Nature is so precious.

We want to preserve our natural habitat.

And that is that!

S4S

This is a tortoise.

A tortoise travels across the terrain

Very, very slowly,

And carries its house on its back.

This territory is a comfortable place for the tortoise.

It suits him to a

You are about to see a very special tree.
It is called the **U**mbrella thorn tree,

With a top as flat as flat can be.
Birds love to rest and nest on high.
And we know why — it's fun to see the sky.

U is for umbrella — you know,
It also keeps you dry,
So if it rains, you won't complain.

We next come to **V**ictoria Falls —
Where the water never stops falling,
And the mists never stop rising.
It's not so surprising.

We're cooled by the spray
All through the day.
V is for a vision we'll carry away.

We hear the warthog before we see him.
His noisy roar announces his coming,
And his footsteps sound almost like drumming.

His snout roots out the food from the ground,
Where vegetables are easily found.
 wants to watch for warthogs!

X marks the spot for our next page
And for our next letter.

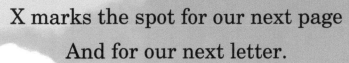

The **X**hosa people of South Africa

Have a tonal language all their own.

When you hear their tongues clicking,

You know they are speaking

Their own special language.

It sounds like music.

Click, click, click.

The yellow–billed stork has feet that are red.

Y stands for yellow,

Its color so mellow.

This bird lives near water and loves to eat fish.

We watch it dive

And come up with its dinner.

This bird is a winner!

Zends our alphabetical safari
And stands for the zebra,
With its stripes of black and white,
It gallops like a horse
And is related to a donkey,
Of course!

Zebras live peacefully in the wild
Eating grasses by rivers and streams.
Ah —
Our safari will live on in our dreams!

And now it's time for Quickly and PanDora
To say a chorus of fond farewells,
And thanks to Ponnie
As they head back home.
No more time to roam.

With a big smile on his face,
Ponnie hands them a parting surprise.
It brings a sparkle to their eyes.
It's a pancake recipe for a South African dish.
As great a dish as they could wish!
And we share it with you, dear readers ...

Happy Pancaking!

Pannekoek

A South African pancake recipe from the kitchen of Jackie Pelletier

Ingredients:

1 cup cake flour
1 teaspoon baking powder
¼ teaspoon salt
1 cup milk
1 cup water
1 egg
2 tablespoons sunflower oil

Preparation:

Sift together the flour, baking powder, and salt.

Beat together the milk, water, egg, and sunflower oil.

Add the milk mixture to the flour mixture and beat until fully mixed.

Chill the batter for an hour.

Heat griddle to medium-high and grease lightly with sunflower oil.

Ladle ¼ cup batter onto hot greased griddle.

Cook until top of pancake bubbles, turn over, and cook until brown.

Keep warm before serving.

Optional:

Sprinkle cinnamon sugar over the pancake and roll up.

Serves 4 – 6

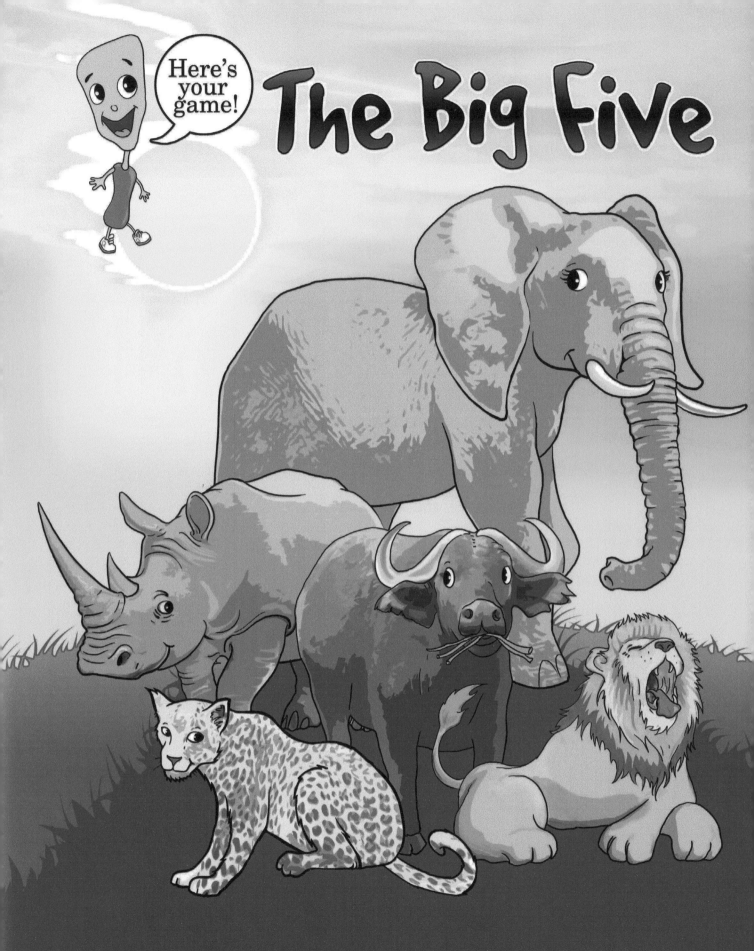

The Big Five

Here's your game!

Can you say their names?

FUN WITH QUICKLY

- Draw a picture of your favorite animal.

- How many Quicklys, that's me, can you find in my book?

- Write or tell a story about an animal.

- Make up a poem or song about an animal.

- How many animals can you help me find in *S is for Safari*?
Please count them all — look closely!

- I hope you will make Ponnie's Pannekoek recipe with your family.

- Here's a matching game:
Write your name.
Match the animals in my book, *S is for Safari,* with the letters of your name.
For example:
If your name is Amy, you will say, "antelope, monkey, yellow-billed stork."

- Please tell me where *you* would like me to go on a future adventure.
You can share your ideas on my website:
QuicklyTheMagicSpatula.com

Your friend,

QUICKLY'S GLOSSARY

Bound: jump

Enormous: very large

Fauna: animal life

Flora: plant life

Frolicking: making merry

Habitat: a place where an animal or plant lives

Humdinger: winner

International: two or more nations

Lair: den

Nattily: neatly dressed

Promenade: to walk around

Roar: a big noise

Terrain: a piece of land

Territory: area

Unwinds: relaxes

Wane: to become smaller in size

Xhosa: A South African tribal nation - pronounced "Kawza"

QUICKLY'S
next adventure
will be
out of
this world!

The Quickly Collection

QUICKLY THE MAGIC SPATULA

Award-winning authors Jeryl Abelmann and Miriam Kronish bring the enchanting story of *Quickly, The Magic Spatula* to life. This childhood memory describes a touching family story. Quickly is rediscovered in a dusty old box in the attic and comes alive in the warmth of Mommy's kitchen.

"This is more than a story about a magic spatula and pancakes. It is about how a simple object can be the source of much joy as it evokes memories of family and growing up." — John R. Grassi, Ph.D., Professor, Cambridge College School of Education

QUICKLY'S MAGICAL PANCAKE ADVENTURE

Quickly's wish is to have a magical pancake adventure — to go out into the world in search of pancake recipes far and wide. This book blends Quickly's adventure with a treasure-trove of delicious pancake recipes.

"My grandchild will love this book."
— Chef Jacques Pépin

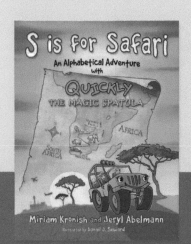

S is for Safari takes Quickly and his friends on an alphabetical journey to South Africa. Join them as they romp through the alphabet from Antelope to Zebra. Readers will delight in the dazzling illustrations and the poetic prose of Quickly's latest adventure.

"A whimsical alphabet-book introduction to the animals of South Africa. Delightful illustrations and rhythmic prose."

— Frances Jacobson Harris, (retired), University Laboratory High School Librarian and Professor Emerita, University of Illinois at Urbana-Champaign

S is for Safari
An Alphabetical Adventure with
QUICKLY THE MAGIC SPATULA

QUICKLY'S Safari Adventure Coloring & Activity Book

Color your way through a South African Safari with Quickly, The Magic Spatula and his friends.

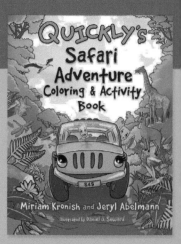

Please visit: DancingMommyPress.com

The Quickly Collection is available online and at your favorite store.